THUMB ON A DIAMOND

THUMB
ON A
DIAMOND

Ken Roberts

·

ILLUSTRATED BY
Leanne Franson

GROUNDWOOD BOOKS / HOUSE OF ANANSI PRESS
TORONTO   BERKELEY

To family.
I have been telling your stories
(only slightly fictionalized)
for many years and have been blessed
to know and learn from all of you.

Groundwood Books / House of Anansi Press
110 Spadina Avenue, Suite 801, Toronto, Ontario M5V 2K4
Distributed in the USA by Publishers Group West
1700 Fourth Street, Berkeley, CA 94710

We acknowledge for their financial support of our publishing
program the Canada Council for the Arts, the Government of Canada
through the Book Publishing Industry Development Program (BPIDP)
and the Ontario Arts Council.

ONTARIO ARTS COUNCIL
CONSEIL DES ARTS DE L'ONTARIO

Library and Archives Canada Cataloguing in Publication
Roberts, Ken
Thumb on a diamond / Ken Roberts; illustrated by Leanne Franson.
ISBN-13: 978-0-88899-629-9 (bound) ISBN-10: 0-88899-629-2 (bound)
ISBN-13: 978-0-88899-705-0 (pbk.) ISBN-10: 0-88899-705-1 (pbk.)
I. Franson, Leanne II. Title.
PS8585.O2968T485 2006   jC813'.54   C2005-907010-2

Printed and bound in Canada

Contents

1

A Foggy Day

THIS is a baseball story, but it seems, when I remember it, to have started the day Mr. Entwhistle arrived.

Most sports stories begin with a game or a race, but this one is different. It starts with a foggy morning.

Susan and I were sitting on the dock, dangling our feet in the water. We heard a rowboat, looked at each other and giggled.

Susan and I had listened to thousands of fishermen row hundreds of dinghies from their anchored boats to our dock at New Auckland, British Columbia. We knew the rhythmic splash that oars make when they are working together.

That was not the sound we heard.

We couldn't see the rowboat or who was trying to guide it to our village. It was too foggy.

"Hello?" called out a man's voice. "Did I hear somebody?"

"Over here," yelled Susan.

"Oh, thank the Lord above," said the man calmly. "Are you on a boat?"

"We're on a dock," I yelled.

"A dock? Land!" The man in the boat stopped rowing and let his dinghy glide forward. He began to laugh.

"Land," he said again.

I could see the bow of the dinghy now, and I could see the misty shape of a man sitting in the middle. The dinghy was drifting closer to us. The rower had swiveled around and was facing us.

"Look," I whispered to Susan, pointing. "Doesn't that man look like…"

"Sherlock Holmes," said Susan slowly.

"Exactly, my dear Susan," I replied, but Susan didn't laugh.

The man in the rowboat was wearing the kind of hat that Sherlock Holmes wears — a hat that looks like a baseball cap with two front ends and flaps that usually tie on the top. It was a damp, cool morning, and the flaps were pulled down over his ears.

The rowboat glided to a stop, gently bumping into the dock. I leaned over, grabbed the bowline and tied the dinghy to a mooring anchor. Susan pulled on the stern line, guiding the boat snug against the dock.

The man stood up, holding onto a gold-tipped cane. He wore a long Burberry coat and smoked a curved white pipe. He wobbled and then placed one hand on the dock and pulled himself up.

"My name is G. H. Entwhistle," he announced. "I am, of course, at your service." He didn't try to shake our hands, but he did bow.

Mr. Entwhistle was tall and thin. His nose was bigger and redder than any nose I had ever seen. His voice was loud, each word precise and accompanied by a broad gesture. He moved like an actor performing in front of thousands of people.

"My name is Susan," said Susan. She bowed slightly, too, so I bowed and said that my name was Thumb.

"Thumb?" asked Mr. Entwhistle.

"My real name is Leon Mazzei but I am called Thumb because I lost the top half of my right thumb in an accident," I said, raising my hand.

"But I can see your entire thumb, Thumb," said Mr. Entwhistle.

"The end is a fake," I said. "I can take it off. You have an accent, Mr. Entwhistle."

"Young lad," said Mr. Entwhistle with a chuckle, pausing as he pulled out a white handkerchief and wiped his forehead. "Everyone has an accent. I, in fact, would find your accent hard to understand if I hadn't been living in this country for seven years."

"Where are you from?" asked Susan.

"England," said Mr. Entwhistle, pointing out into the fog. "It is hard for me to say that I am actually from England, since I have not seen the sacred soil of my beloved country for too many years. It's my work. It brings me here, alas. If only I had chosen some lovable English creature such as the dormouse, I might not have faced near doom today on this almost uninhabited coast of British Columbia. Not that I was frightened for a moment, you understand. I am English and was taught from an early age that one should never show fear."

"Why?" asked Susan.

"I don't know. I only know that I am more frightened by what might happen if I show fear than by any fearful thing I might face. My boat seems to have sunk. I barely had time to change clothes so that I could be dressed in the way I might want to be found if this were the end. Where am I, by the way?"

I had seen many frightened fishermen and women, mostly after they had found their way home after a sudden winter storm. The frightened people I had seen were shaking and mumbling. Mr. Entwhistle was the first person I had ever seen whose boat had actually sunk during a storm. Mr. Entwhistle looked crisp and elegant.

"You are in New Auckland," I said.

"I thought I knew all the fishing villages along the coast," he said, frowning.

"We're small," said Susan. "Only 138 people

live here, unless Mrs. Hartog had her baby last night. We have forty-two buildings, including the school, the garage and the basketball arena."

"A garage! So there is a road. I can perhaps pay someone to give me a ride to Prince Rupert so that I might quickly fly away."

"No," said Susan. "There's no road. We're surrounded by mountains. And the ocean, of course."

"But you have a garage," he said, as if he was trying to convince us that there was a road and we had just forgotten.

"It's not really a garage," I said. "We use it to store things."

"You have boats, though? And a telephone?"

"We have lots of boats and several phones."

"Ah, splendid. I need to make a call. I hit some rocks in the fog and was lucky enough to find your village. I still have to call the Coast Guard. There is a bright side to this ordeal. I was the only occupant and I am safe."

"You can come up to my house," I said. "My dad's the school principal. We have a phone."

Susan and I led Mr. Entwhistle down the dock and onto the sand. Susan and I walked slowly at first, figuring that anyone with a cane might need a little more time, but Mr. Entwhistle didn't use his cane to help him walk. He swung it casually over his shoulder and then swung it back and tapped it on the ground like Fred Astaire in one of those old dance movies.

We crossed the sand to the cedar sidewalk that runs along the first row of houses. The houses are clumped close together, like they're protecting each other from the damp. A few houses actually seem to lean toward each other to stay warm. All the houses have windows facing the sidewalk.

As we passed each house, people glanced up from doing dishes or reading books or fixing fishing gear. Nobody was surprised to see Susan or me, but they were surprised to see Mr. Entwhistle. No boat or plane had landed, but here we were, leading a stranger down the boardwalk − a stranger who looked like a famous storybook detective seen on the foggy streets of London, England.

"You look like a detective," I said. "Are you?"

"No. I am a writer and an artist. I am Gerald Entwhistle. Perhaps you've heard of me?"

"I don't think so," said Susan.

"Me, either," I said. "But we're only twelve."

"Ah, but it is children for whom I write and paint. I am the author and illustrator of the Bobby and Bernice Beaver books."

"I read one of those," I said excitedly. "Bobby and his wife Bernice are beavers who build dams that look like famous buildings."

"You have it, my lad," said Mr. Entwhistle, patting my head, which is something I usually hate. "And for my art I must travel this beaver-laden country and draw the little beasts in their habitat."

"Couldn't you just go to the zoo in London or something?" asked Susan. "They've got beavers there, right?"

"Yes, but I pride myself in the accuracy of my drawings. I need the natural flowers and trees where beaver live. I need the proper hue of the water and the texture of the rocks. I am a perfectionist, you see. Animals must be drawn in their proper environment."

A loud, deep roar seemed to make the fog swirl in front of us. The sound echoed off the mountains.

Mr. Entwhistle stopped.

"What was that?" he asked, his voice quiet for the first time. He didn't sound afraid, just curious.

"A lion," I said casually.

"A mountain lion? It's close," he added, puffing more quickly on his pipe. He sent round balls of smoke into the air like miniature smoke signals.

"It's an African lion," I said. "She's not in her natural habitat. She's locked in the tennis court and she's hungry."

"You have a lion in this village?" asked Mr. Entwhistle. He said it calmly, but he did take a small step back toward his rowboat.

"Yes," said Susan. "Muriel was left here when she was a cub. She's our pet now. She's tame."

"Imagine that," said Mr. Entwhistle. "I am in

a Canadian west coast village with a tame lion. Ah, life is strange. This morning I stared death in the eye," he said, like a stage actor overplaying his part, "and now I share this fine little village with an African lion. We are both poor souls far from home."

"Here's my house," I said, stopping on the wooden walkway. "Come on in."

2

Welcome

Dad was sitting at the kitchen table, talking on the phone. There weren't many phones in the village. The mountains blocked the satellites some of the time.

Dad glanced up and stared in surprise as Mr. Entwhistle stepped through the door behind us. Then he hung up, fast.

My dad is bald and always wears a tie. He owns the only three ties in the village. He's the only person who has ever worn a tie, except for the time that the queen's yacht, *Britannia*, passed by our coast a few years ago with the queen herself on board. She'd taken a trip up to the Queen Charlotte Islands to see the totem poles and was heading down to Vancouver. We all hopped on fishing boats and headed out to greet her, riding the waves and standing on the decks of our convoy.

Dad had loaned the two ties he wasn't wearing to the mayor and the mayor's wife. We all waved and *Britannia* tooted out a response. I don't think the queen, if she was watching, noticed the ties. It was a rainy day and everyone's parkas were zipped.

"Pardon my intrusion," said Mr. Entwhistle, removing his Sherlock Holmes hat and holding it in one hand. "Your son and his lovely friend invited me to your charming home, sir, so that I might ask permission to use your phone. It seems that my boat has sunk to the bottom of the deep blue sea. I was lucky enough to escape in my dinghy and to find safe haven in your fine community."

"In this fog?" asked Dad as he glanced outside.

"Yes. Indeed. It was the fog that caused me to sink. I hit some rocks."

"You're lucky to be alive," said Dad. "Sure. Use the phone. The Coast Guard emergency number is on the wall above the kitchen counter."

Mr. Entwhistle made his call.

Our kitchen is part of the living-room. The

only other rooms in our house are the two small bedrooms and the bathroom. The bedroom walls don't go all the way to the ceiling so the heat can circulate. The bathroom is the only room that's completely private.

Dad, Susan and I stepped outside so Mr. Entwhistle could talk in private.

"They just won't listen," said Dad.

"Who won't listen to what?" I asked, although I was pretty sure I knew what he was talking about.

Dad really wanted to take a bunch of kids to Vancouver so we could see cars and elevators and tall buildings. The school board wouldn't pay for the field trip. It was too expensive.

I know some schools ask students to sell chocolate bars so they can raise money for school trips, but there are only 138 people in our whole village. We'd be awfully fat if we had to eat enough chocolate to pay for trips and library books and computers.

"I just can't convince the school board that it is important for children to see the broader world," said Dad.

Susan sighed. She had never been to any city larger than Prince Rupert. I had been to Vancouver lots of times and even to Toronto and Seattle, but I hadn't been anywhere for a couple of years.

The door opened and Mr. Entwhistle peeked out at us.

"You didn't have to leave," he said. "It is your house."

We all went back inside. I figured we had about five minutes before friends started to knock on the door, wondering about the stranger.

"The Coast Guard will search when the fog lifts," said Mr. Entwhistle, shaking his head sadly. He asked if he could sit and then did, heavily. "I think they are far more interested in making sure that no wreckage gets into the shipping lanes."

"Your boat can't be far," said Dad. "We'll find it and salvage what we can. I'm surprised you made it here. There isn't another shack or village for thirty kilometers up or down the coast. It's a miracle."

But Mr. Entwhistle wasn't really listening. He was staring at one of the cedar walls. He suddenly stood up, walked to the wall, reached into his pocket and pulled out a small leather case. He opened the case, carefully took out some glasses and set them on his nose. He stared at a large painting of mountains on a misty morning. He inspected every inch of it before glancing down at the corner to see the signature.

"This painting," he said. "Is it an original Annie Pritchard?"

"Yes," said Dad.

"You bought it?"

"Annie gave it to me for Christmas one year."

"Annie Pritchard gave you one of her paintings?" Mr. Entwhistle asked, making it sound like the queen had given us her crown jewels.

"Yes."

Mr. Entwhistle removed his glasses, put them away and sat back down on the couch, still staring at the painting.

"It's beautiful," he said. "One of her best. I

know she maintains a cottage somewhere on this coast but she could live anywhere. She's one of the most famous painters in the world. I went to an exhibit of her work at the Tate Gallery in London."

Before Dad could tell Mr. Entwhistle that Annie lived next door, Charlie Semanov, our mayor when we needed one (which wasn't often), opened the door and poked his head inside. He spotted Mr. Entwhistle and then pulled his head back outside and closed the door.

I glanced out the window. People were standing in front of our house, staring at the door. Village houses are built close to the sidewalk. We walk in front of them so much that it is considered impolite to stare into anyone's windows. Big Charlie was talking excitedly.

The fog was lifting. I could even see the bottom slopes of mountains across the basin. Another crowd down by the dock was looking at Mr. Entwhistle's rowboat. I could see people shielding their eyes from the glare of the thin fog as they searched the bay for a larger boat that didn't belong to anyone in the village.

Our door opened again and Big Charlie held it open so people could tramp inside.

"This is Mr. Gerald Entwhistle," said Dad, standing up. "His boat sank."

"Are you a fisherman?" asked Big Charlie Semanov in his booming voice.

Big Charlie was a man who liked to hug people. He hugged people on their birthdays and even for catching a big fish. I knew that he wanted to rush over and hug this man for having lost his boat because to a fisherman, losing a boat is almost as bad as losing a family member. But he also needed to find out if this stranger had been trying to catch the fish along our shore. Big Charlie and some of the other fishermen seemed to think that anyone fishing in our bay was like a cattle rustler, even though our fish weren't branded.

"No," said Mr. Entwhistle. "I am not a fisherman. I'm an Englishman."

"Would you like a cup of coffee?" Dad asked Mr. Entwhistle.

"Yes. Please," said Mr. Entwhistle, turning his head to nod.

It was a shame that Mr. Entwhistle turned his head. He didn't see Big Charlie race across the room, his arms outstretched like a football player. He didn't see Big Charlie until it was impossible not to see Big Charlie since Mr. Entwhistle's entire body was surrounded by nothing but Big Charlie.

Big Charlie hugged him. I heard Mr. Entwhistle mumble something and noticed that his shoes weren't touching the ground.

Big Charlie let go. Then he slapped Mr. Entwhistle on the back so hard that the poor man almost fell over.

"What was her name?" asked Big Charlie.

"My...boat?" asked Mr. Entwhistle, trying to catch his breath.

"Yes."

"*Bernice,*" said Mr. Entwhistle.

"Ah," said Big Charlie, nodding. "Named after your mother, your wife, or your daughter?"

"A beaver," said Mr. Entwhistle. "An imaginary beaver."

"Coffee's ready," said Dad, setting a cup on

our table as Big Charlie scratched his head. Big Charlie had never heard of a boat named for an imaginary anything and didn't quite know what to say.

When Mr. Entwhistle had finished his coffee, Big Charlie invited him to step outside and take a look at the village. The crowd behind Big Charlie Semanov was beginning to break up. I could hear the diesel engines of fishing boats fire up. Horns sounded, with special beeps telling crew members to get down to the dock. The fishing boats would be leaving soon.

Susan and I sauntered along behind Big Charlie and Mr. Entwhistle as they retraced our steps. Annie Pritchard stood on the dock, leaning on her cane and staring out at the mountains across the sound. Big Charlie slapped Mr. Entwhistle on the back again and announced that he had to go and check his boat. Mr. Entwhistle walked up close to Annie.

"Are you watching the boats leave?" asked Mr. Entwhistle. "Do you have a husband or a son or daughter on one of them?"

"I have no relatives on any of those boats,"

said Annie calmly. "But I do have many friends. Today I am here just to stare at the mountains as they emerge from the fog. It is a sight I have seen thousands of times but love more every day. I can tell you which trees and rocks and streams will be revealed next, as the fog thins. The uncovering still delights me. By the way, I'm Annie. You are that fellow whose boat sank, right?"

"Indeed," said Mr. Entwhistle. "Gerald Entwhistle."

Mr. Entwhistle asked Annie the name of one of the craggy, twisted peaks across the bay.

"That's Roger's Mount," Annie answered. "It was named after my grandfather because he was the first person to climb it. He didn't climb it for any particular reason. He just hated not knowing what was on the other side."

"Do you ever wonder what's on the other side?"

Annie laughed. "No. I like to make up what might be on the other side. I don't need facts. Facts just get in the way."

Mr. Entwhistle asked Annie the names of

three waterfalls, two valleys between peaks and a huge rock perched on the side of Roger's Mount. He asked about a small, blue-ice glacier. Annie knew the names of everything and at least three stories about each.

"Are there any beaver around here?" asked Mr. Entwhistle.

"Oh, my, yes," said Annie, laughing. "They're in all the bogs around the bay. When the snow melts, it runs down the cliffs and settles into craters along the shore. We get our water from a pond halfway up the mountain behind us. We have to stop beaver from building in the pond about once a month. Can't have them living in our drinking water, you know."

"So, a person could see plenty of beaver just by riding around the bay in a rowboat?"

"Yes. Of course."

Mr. Entwhistle thanked her, tipped his hat, backed away from the dock and slowly walked through the village, humming.

After about an hour he came back to the dock and asked Big Charlie Semanov if the Addison house, which was empty, was for sale.

"There's not much room in our village," said Big Charlie, barely paying attention as he inspected a fishing net hung to dry. "We've got a mountain behind us and the ocean in front. There's only room for so many buildings. But most of the young people don't stay. They go to Prince Rupert and work there. Nobody can sell you that empty house because there aren't any records down in Victoria to say who owns which piece of our beach. Our village is listed as a company and the company owns the village. It's easier that way."

Big Charlie turned and inspected Mr. Entwhistle with the same eye he used when he was looking for flaws in his nets.

"Tell you what," he said at last. "Fix the Addison house and you can stay as long as you want. You can't buy it but you can't sell it when you leave, either. Any improvements you make will have to stay with the house. Fair?"

"Fair."

"Tell me, though. This morning you were anxious to get away from here as fast as you could. Now you want to buy a house and stay.

You might want to wait another hour or two. Maybe you'll change your mind again," said Big Charlie with a chuckle.

"I'll tell you why I want to stay," said Mr. Entwhistle. "I'm not homesick here. It surprises me, really. I've been homesick for years. I always thought that I was homesick for my country but I realized, talking to that woman earlier, that I have been homesick for the way the people in my part of England feel about the countryside around them."

Mr. Entwhistle told Charlie that he had been raised in the Lake District of England, a place where every hill and every pond and grove of trees has a name and has had a name for hundreds of years. Mr. Entwhistle liked Canada, except for the fact that there are so many mountains that hills are rarely named, and so many lakes and rivers that creeks and ponds don't seem to count.

"Even mountains," he said, "may have names on official maps stored in an Ottawa basement, but they are just part of the scenery to people who stare at them every day. I like your village. Every piece of scenery has a name and a history. It reminds me of home."

So, Mr. Entwhistle moved into the Addison house and discovered that the woman at the dock was an artist even more famous than him.

I promised you a baseball story, but I wanted you to have some sense of our village first. You may have noticed something. If you didn't, I'll make it clear. There is no grass in New Auckland. There is no field in New Auckland. Our tiny group of buildings hugs the sandy shore between a tall, rocky mountain and the deep, salty ocean.

This is not an ordinary baseball story.

3

The Idea

SKIP...skip...skip...skip...plop.
The skips were the sounds of a small flat stone jumping across the ocean's surface, away from the beach. The plop was the sound of that same stone sinking.

"Four skips," I yelled to Susan. "I'm pathetic."

"A wave must have hit it," said Susan. She leaned over and started to search the rocky beach. She picked up four flat rocks, checked their size and weight, and dropped three back onto the beach. She stared out at the ocean, concentrating. She pulled back her arm and flipped the stone over the water.

"One...two...three...four...five...six...seven..." I counted out loud before the stone disappeared under the water's surface. "You win."

Susan always won.

"Do you think people all over the world skip stones when there's water around?" I asked.

"Maybe people all over the world aren't as bored as we are," suggested Susan.

"We could fish off the dock."

"Like we did yesterday and the day before?"

"We could play a board game."

"Every game in the village has at least three missing pieces."

I listened to the soft waves lap onto the beach. Even the ocean was lazy and bored.

"What I really want," said Susan, sitting on the rocky beach, "is to go someplace. I want to go to Vancouver or Toronto or Seattle or New York or Paris or even Prince Rupert. I want to see an elevator. I want to see streetlights and a real park with swings. I want that school trip your dad keeps talking about."

"He's trying," I said. "He's written tons of letters, and he talks to people at the school board for a few hours each week."

"And?"

I shrugged. "There's money for sports

teams and for tournaments but there isn't any money for a group of kids to just see a city."

New Auckland has a basketball team for the high-school kids. All the villages along the coast love basketball and have good teams. Sometimes our team manages to win the league championship and go to the regional championships and even to the provincial championships in Vancouver.

None of the villages have teams for other sports.

"What if we had a sports team?" asked Susan. "Then we could become champions and the school board would have to pay for us to go to Vancouver."

"Nobody from this village plays anything except basketball. And you have to be in high school to play on the team. Besides, the basketball season doesn't even start until next fall."

"What about some other sport?"

"What sport?"

"Well, we've got nine kids in grades six to nine, counting the ones who commute from cabins along the coast. Football takes eleven on each side and the equipment costs a lot. You need twelve kids for soccer. Besides, soccer takes a lot of running around and Big Bette and Little Liam won't play any sport if they have to run too much."

Big Bette is actually quite small and Little Liam is huge but the word Big sounds better in front of Bette and the word Little sounds better in front of Liam. Dad says we're using irony, which is something he's been trying to teach us at school.

"What sport?" I asked again.

"Baseball," whispered Susan.

I laughed. "Even if we had a team," I said, "and even if the school board was willing to pay for a team to go to the championships, we'd have to beat all the other villages. I don't think we could beat anybody. Have you ever played baseball?"

"You know I haven't. I've lived here my entire life. Do you know how to play?"

"Sort of. I know there are three outs for each team in an inning..."

"What's an inning?"

"...and I know most of the ways a person can get out and I know there are three bases plus home plate. I know something else," I said, grinning and wiggling my eyebrows.

"What?"

"I know that there are a few bats and some gloves in the school equipment room."

We ran to the gym. We moved mats and basketballs until we found three bats, seven gloves and a box with twelve new baseballs. The school board probably sent the same collection of sports equipment to all the schools, even the ones with no grass or fields.

We tried on gloves, found ones that sort of fit, grabbed the bats and a couple of balls and ran down to the beach.

We stood about five paces apart and started to throw the ball back and forth. Most of the time the ball would hit one of our gloves and fall out before we could squeeze the pocket closed.

"Why do we need gloves?" asked Susan. "Why don't we just use our hands?"

"I think the ball travels a lot faster when somebody hits it."

"Let's try."

Susan picked up one of the bats, the smallest, and held it on her shoulder. I tossed the ball toward her. She swung, far too late, and the ball rolled down the beach behind her. We tried again and again, but Susan kept missing and then dropping the bat and running to pick up the ball. When Susan threw me the ball I could usually manage to make it land in my mitt but I couldn't seem to close the mitt in time. Most of the time the ball flopped out and stopped on the beach close to my feet. Sometimes I had to chase it.

Susan looked at me and said, "We're really bad."

"We've just never played before," I said. "Most kids in cities practice throwing and catching and hitting. We'd probably laugh at them if we ever saw them trying to row a boat."

"So we have to form a team but not play anybody. The other villages in our school league won't bother because none of their kids play baseball, either. We'll win the league championship by default and the school board will have to pay for us to go to Vancouver."

"But when we get to Vancouver, there will be teams that really can play baseball."

"We won't play them, Thumb."

"Why not?"

"Well, we couldn't be expected to play if one or two of us happen to get sick. We'll just tour the city for a couple of days and come home."

"Dad will never go for it."

"Why not?"

"You're planning to cheat. Dad's the principal, and teachers and principals are not supposed to encourage kids to cheat."

"So? We won't tell him. I mean, we'll tell him about forming a team and challenging the other villages and we'll practice, which might even be fun. But when we get to Vancouver he'll think that a couple of us got sick and he'll be happy because he just wants to get us to the city anyway."

"We'll need to get all the kids to agree first."

Susan thought for a moment.

"You're right," she said. "Round them up and I'll meet you all in the gym."

4

The Team

ROBBIE was easy to find because he was almost always at home. Robbie was a grade six kid with really short hair. Every Saturday morning his dad plopped a chair out on the sidewalk. Robbie came out bundled in his winter coat in cold weather or holding an umbrella if it was raining. He sat down and his dad quickly ran hair clippers over Robbie's head. It didn't take long since Robbie's hair never seemed to grow during the week.

After his weekly haircut Robbie never even wiggled around trying to stop little hairs from itching his back. Most of us figured there were no little hairs. We decided Robbie was bald and the weekly haircuts were done so that he could pretend he had hair to cut.

Robbie was not an athlete. He liked those role-playing strategy games that take hours to move miniature figures across living-room carpets littered with kitchen pots and cups that are supposed to be mountains and villages. When you walked past his house you could hear him making battle noises with his mouth. He was really good. It sounded like a real battle was taking place in his living-room.

Robbie was in his living-room, of course. I knocked and he answered the door.

"Hey, Thumb," said Robbie excitedly. "I was just about to reenact the Battle of Goliath Swamp from the fifth book of the Cliff Holt series. Do you want to play? You can be the demonic giants if you want. They win."

"Actually," I said, "I was wondering if you want to take a trip down to Vancouver?"

Robbie glanced down toward the dock, half expecting to see some boat getting ready to leave.

"Right now?" he asked.

"No. On a field trip for school. It won't happen for a couple of months."

"Well, sure. There are some terrific miniatures stores in Vancouver and kids play on special tables that are designed to look like forts and mountains and forests. But shouldn't your dad be asking my dad or something?"

"My dad doesn't know. Not yet. Susan has a plan. We're meeting in the gym in about a half hour. See you there, okay?"

"Sure."

I waved and ran toward the beach where kids were sorting stones by color and size and then hauling them by wheelbarrow to Mr. Entwhistle's house.

Mr. Entwhistle was transforming the old Addison house into an English cottage that looked like a hobbit home. He'd taken the old door and rounded it at the top, steaming some cedar and curving it so that the top of the doorway was rounded to fit the door. He'd also molded driftwood around the two front windows and was building a chimney made from small stones and rocks mortared together. I figured the house was going to look like the third house built by one of the three little pigs.

Big Bette was sorting stones for the walls.

Big Bette was so small herself that she could

probably have run through the legs of most kids her age without slowing down. Big Bette loved horses, although she'd never seen a real horse. She liked to run on all fours and pretend to be a horse. She ran like that boy in the Jungle Book cartoon, the one raised by wolves. She could really move fast.

"Susan's got a plan for getting all of us to Vancouver," I said. "We're all going to meet in the gym."

"When?" she asked, tossing a pinkish stone onto a pile.

"Thirty minutes. Can you tell the others?"

"Sure," she said, dropping to all fours. "I'll just pretend I'm the Pony Express."

She galloped off, neighing and snorting and occasionally kicking up her back legs. When she pretended to be a horse, she was always a spirited one.

We met in the gym. The kids we'd rounded up sat in the stands while Susan and I stood in front. I held a bat on my shoulder with a glove looped over it like I'd seen in some movie.

The only one of us who could be called an

athlete was Nick, who was in grade seven. Nick was the best basketball player in the school. He practiced every day, whenever he wasn't on a fishing boat. Most of the time he had to practice by himself, dribbling down the court and weaving past make-believe defenders, turning to reach over invisible arms as he shot.

Susan explained her plan. I volunteered to be one of the kids who got sick.

"Heck," I said. "If I'm sick then I can stay in the hotel room and watch a real television with real stations." We had two televisions in New Auckland but we could only watch movies. No television signals made it over our mountains.

Robbie raised his hand.

"Yes," said Susan, pointing at him like she was a teacher.

"Can I be sick, too? I'm really good at pretending to be sick. My dad thinks I get sick way more than I really do."

The rest of us stared at Robbie. He did get sick a lot.

"What if we actually do play?" asked Big Bette.

"Play what?" I asked.

"Play the baseball games down in Vancouver."

"I could tell you one thing that would happen, for sure," I said.

"What?" asked Big Bette.

"We'd lose."

"Why?"

"Have you ever played baseball?"

"You know I haven't. I've lived here my entire life."

"Down in the city," I said, "there's grass and there's space between the houses and parks where kids can catch and throw and hit baseballs for hours a day, kind of like the way you practice basketball, Nick. We can't beat any of the other teams. Never."

"Actually," said Susan slowly. "I stopped by my house just before we all met and I checked on the Internet. If we did play, we wouldn't have to finish any of the games. The tournament uses a rule called the mercy rule. If, after two innings, any team is losing by more than ten runs, then the game is declared over so that the team being massacred doesn't have to be totally embarrassed. Besides, it's a double knockout tournament and that means a team goes home after losing two games. So if we did play, we'd only play four innings of baseball."

"What's an inning?" asked Robbie.

"An inning," said Susan, "is when both teams have had a chance to bat and each team has successfully stopped the other team from batting by completing three outs," said Susan. "I looked up the rules. In professional games, teams play nine innings. Teams play seven-inning games in this tournament."

"So, we'd still have to play well enough to get at least six batters out before this mercy rule stops a game?" asked Nick.

"Yeah," I said.

"Why is the ball so small?" asked Big Bette. "I mean, the ball would be easier to hit if it was big."

"A golf ball is a lot smaller," I said.

"Yeah," said Little Liam, "but a golf ball stays still when you hit it. A baseball comes at you. It's moving."

Dad says Little Liam is so big he probably wants to be a boat when he grows up, maybe even a ship. I had to sit behind Little Liam at school one year, at least until the first report cards. The teacher wrote that I never raised my hand or volunteered for anything. I told her that I raised my hand all the time but she just couldn't see it. She moved Little Liam to the back row and gave him her desk and chair so he had enough room to sit.

"Well," said Susan, "I don't think we're going to be able to rewrite the rules of baseball. We'd have to use the ball that already exists."

"How can we learn to hit?" asked Nick. "If we practice and we do hit a baseball it will either hit somebody's house or fly into the ocean. We don't have enough room."

"I thought about that, too," said Susan. "We can practice throwing and catching in here, in the gym. And we can practice running to the bases, too. We can practice hitting outside. We'll string some fishing nets around the batting area so the net will stop the ball. We'll leave an opening between the batter and the pitcher and put some more nets behind the pitcher's mound."

"I don't know . . . " said Nick.

"If we're going to go to Vancouver as a baseball team," I said, "shouldn't we learn a little bit about how to play baseball?"

"We're going to stink," said Nick, bouncing his basketball a couple of times, which is something he does when he's trying to think.

"But we're kids," I said. "Let's play baseball, just like other kids."

"Yeah," Nick said slowly. "You're right. Let's practice hard. And then, the night before we're supposed to play our first game, let's meet and decide if anybody's going to get sick or if we'll actually play."

I figured Nick had been watching too many sports movies. The ones where a team of losers wins the championship game.

5

Practice

I COOKED dinner for Dad that night. I always cooked dinner when I told Dad what I wanted for Christmas or when I wanted a friend to sleep overnight. I made spaghetti with a sauce that came from a can but I cooked the noodles right. They weren't chewy and they weren't soggy.

Dad and I had lived in New Auckland for three years. We moved here the year after Mom died. Some people, when they lose somebody they love, want to stay in the same house and walk down the same streets. It helps them to remember.

Dad couldn't stand sleeping in the same room where he and Mom had slept. He couldn't stand shopping in the same grocery store. He needed to move, and he needed to move to some place that was completely different. He used to say that the funny thing is that he loves New Auckland and keeps thinking that Mom would have loved it, too.

"So. What's up?" asked Dad. "I didn't get a free spaghetti dinner for nothing."

"Susan and I figured out how to get all of us to Vancouver and how to get the school board to pay."

I twirled my spaghetti and took a bite. Dad did, too.

"There has to be a catch," he said, "or you wouldn't have made me dinner."

Dad took another bite and stared at me over the top of his glasses.

"We want to play baseball at the provincial championships," I said as calmly as possible. I even looked at Dad and tried a confident smile.

I don't think it looked too confident. I don't even think it looked much like a smile

"Who is us?" asked Dad.

"All the kids in the middle grades."

"Baseball? None of you knows how to play baseball. There isn't even a place to practice."

"No other village has a place to play, either.

We challenge them and then we'll win since nobody will play us and we'll all go to the provincial championships."

"Why would you want to play at the provincial championships?"

"Because the championships are held in Vancouver, Dad. We can all go to Vancouver and the school board will have to pay."

"Oh."

Dad sat back in his chair and stared out the front window. I am not too good with directions but I think he was actually staring toward Vancouver.

"But you'll have to play baseball at some point," said Dad at last. "Your first game will never end unless the other team just gets tired of scoring and helps put themselves out."

"Susan checked. If a team is ahead by more than ten runs after two innings, then the game is automatically over. Dad, you want to get all of us to Vancouver. We want to go to Vancouver. Our plan will take us there. Besides, we're going to practice. We'll make sure we know how to catch and hit and run, even if we do it badly."

"Practice? Where? The first ball that somebody hits will either break a window or land in the ocean. You can't practice baseball on a narrow beach full of houses."

"We're going to put up nets."

Dad tilted his head and frowned. He only does that when he's trying to read my brain, as if it's easier to look right inside my head when he looks at me from a slightly different angle.

"You guys aren't planning to win any of these games or anything stupid like that, are you?"

"Dad," I said calmly, looking him right in the eyes. "We know we can't win. We just want to see Vancouver. You're the one who got everybody excited about seeing a city, and we figured out a way to make it happen. And you know what? We just want to do something that kids in other towns do every day. We just want to run on grass and play some baseball."

"You've got a whole team?"

"Yeah. Everybody in grade six to grade eight. We found some gloves and balls and bats in the gym equipment room."

"I'll tell you what," said Dad, taking another bite of spaghetti. "If you guys practice, then I'll challenge the other villages in our league. And if you keep practicing, I'll tell the school board that we're the coastal villages champions and have a right to attend the provincial championships. Okay?"

"Yeah."

* * *

Susan figured out that we could make room to pitch a ball the right distance if we put the pitcher's mound between my house and Annie's house. We put the batter's box next to the fire truck. First base was across the sand by the garage.

We dragged some old net up from the docks, and Little Liam nailed it up between my house and Annie's. He left an opening so that the batter could run to first base after hitting the ball. The only problem was that first base was off to the left, and in a real baseball game first base is off to the right.

"All right," said Susan when we were

finished. "Who wants to bat and who wants to pitch?"

"I'll bat," said Big Bette, "but the bats we have are way too big for me."

"Any bat is going to be too big for you," said Susan, "but that's a good thing. It will help us. You're the only one who doesn't have to take batting practice."

Big Bette frowned. "Why?"

"The pitcher has to throw at least three strikes to each batter, unless the batter swings. Strikes are pitches that are over the home plate and between a batter's knees and shoulders. The pitcher's target changes with each player. A tall player has a big strike zone and a shorter player like you has a small strike zone. A pitcher has to be really accurate with a small player."

Big Bette grinned. "So what happens if the pitcher can't throw strikes? Do we get a point?"

"No. And baseball doesn't have points. It counts runs."

"What's a run worth, then?"

"Basically, one point. But baseball calls that point a run."

"Why?"

"I don't know, but I do know that if the pitcher throws four pitches that aren't in the strike zone before throwing three strikes, then you get to walk calmly to first base and become a base runner. If we play, you're going to be a base runner a lot so you should find out what a base runner can do."

Big Bette didn't say anything for a moment. "Doesn't a base runner just run between bases?" she asked. "That's what they do in movies."

"Sure," said Susan. "But a base runner has to know the right times to run and the right times to stop. Like you can run to second base if somebody gets a hit. Or you can actually steal second base."

"Can I keep it?" asked Big Bette seriously.

"Keep what?"

"Second base."

"When?"

"When I steal it. Or do I have to give it back? And what are we going to do with a second base after I steal it? And how can we keep playing if there is no second base? Are there spares?"

"I think you'd better read the rule book," said Susan.

Susan reached into her backpack and pulled out a binder of rules that she had printed from the Internet.

"Who wants to bat?" I asked again.

"I will," said Nick.

"And I'll pitch," said a voice behind us. We all turned. My dad stood between the houses holding a baseball glove.

"But...you're an adult."

"And if you're going to play, it would probably be a good idea if you didn't look too stupid out there," said Dad. "The players who are going to be pitchers can't learn to pitch during batting practice. They'll throw so many pitches that their arms will get sore. I'll pitch batting practice because I have actually played baseball before and can probably throw balls fairly similar to the ones you'll have to hit down in Vancouver. Meanwhile, half of you go down to the beach so that your pitching coach can teach you a few things about throwing."

"Our pitching coach?"

"Me," said Mr. Entwhistle, peeking between the houses. He was dressed completely in white, with long sleeves and pants that looked pressed and cleaned. He wore a white cap that looked like a short-billed baseball hat.

"I have never played baseball," he announced happily, "but I was a smashingly good cricket player and it is almost the same thing. In both games you toss a ball and you hit a ball and you run between bases. I have only one question."

"What?" I asked.

"What's an inning?" said Mr. Entwhistle, and then, thankfully, he laughed.

Down on the beach, Mr. Entwhistle had us line up.

"I understand that baseball is different from cricket," he said. "In cricket, the person tossing the ball can take a running start. Besides, he tries to hit the wickets behind the batsman, not aim for a catcher's mitt."

"Mr. Entwhistle," I said, raising my hand.

"Yes, Thumb."

"I think we're going to have a hard enough

time learning baseball without learning the differences between baseball and cricket."

"Fine point, lad. By the way, if you take off that thumb of yours, maybe you can find a funny way to hold the ball and make it curve. I've heard that some pitchers can curve the ball by holding it oddly."

I can't really take off my thumb. Big Charlie's son came to build our garage last summer, and he brought a joke to town. He said his thumb had been amputated in an accident and that he had a fake thumb. He turned his back to his audience and slid his healthy thumb through a hole in the bottom of a cardboard jewelry box and laid it on top of a bed of cotton. He showed people his thumb, lying in its tiny coffin. And then, just when everyone was leaning over close and feeling sorry for him, Big Charlie's son wiggled his thumb.

People cracked their heads together, they moved back so fast. They yelled and screamed. Most of the village ran down to the dock to see what was wrong.

When Big Charlie's son wiggled his thumb

for me, I backed up so fast that I fell off the dock.

After Big Charlie's son left, the village decided that it didn't want the joke to leave with him and that I was the one who had to have an accident and be called Thumb so that any visitor could be scared and the whole village could laugh. Annie Pritchard carved me a wooden box with a hole on the bottom and most people who see the carved box are so stunned that they never question my story about a thumb amputation and being able to take my fake thumb off with screws.

I hadn't wiggled my thumb for Mr. Entwhistle. Not yet. But people were already making bets about how he would react.

"I wouldn't be able to hold a baseball without my thumb," I said to Mr. Entwhistle. I held up my hand and wiggled all my fingers and my thumb.

"I suppose not," said Mr. Entwhistle, disappointed. "Now, none of you has the time necessary to learn how to throw fastballs. But I found a book in the school library on how to throw something called junk. Junk pitches are pitches that curve or fall or slide or move in some way that makes the ball hard to hit or, when hit, make it hard for the batters to hit well. I have some pictures of grips that will make the ball curve and twist."

I thought about what Mr. Entwhistle said and then glanced at the book.

"What if we don't think about pitching baseballs at all," I said slowly. "We've never thrown baseballs. But we have tossed stones. What if we use that same motion to throw baseballs instead of rocks? We might be pretty good."

"But we choose stones that are flat," said Robbie. "Round rocks don't spin."

"Round rocks don't spin because there's no good place to grip them," I said. "Baseballs have seams, places where the stitches are raised on the surface. We can use the seams to make the baseballs spin."

"Excellent," said Mr. Entwhistle.

"There are a couple of problems," I said.

"Such as?"

"We never have to aim at anything when we skip stones. All we have to do is hit the ocean."

6

Six Weeks Later

I WOKE up early the day we sailed to Vancouver. I put some wood in the stove and heated some water while Dad quietly dressed and checked our duffle bags. We ate breakfast — a couple of slices of dried salmon wrapped in bread and a cup of tea. Neither of us spoke since we were both struggling to wake up. We slipped on our coats, grabbed our bags and walked down to the dock.

Most mornings, when the fishing boats are getting ready to leave, you can hear people talking and laughing as they make their way down to the dock. Dad and I saw Big Bette and others close their front doors and pick up their bags and head for the boats, everyone glancing back at their homes. Most kids had never left the village, never slept in another bed. I don't know why everyone else was so quiet but I do know why I was.

I was at least a little bit scared.

Our baseball team met just after dawn. We took three dinghies out to *The Golden Maiden*, Big Charlie Semanov's boat. He winched up the anchor and powered out through the channel to the open sea.

Logging companies haul thousands of logs down the coast to paper and sawmills. They herd the logs together like cattle and then fasten the outside logs together, creating a gigantic raft bigger than our entire village.

Each log boom is attached by cable to a tugboat. The biggest booms use tugboats large enough for passengers to hitch rides down to the city. Big Charlie had called a few of the logging companies by radio and found a tug that was traveling empty. He managed to talk them into letting our team ride.

Tugboats that haul booms have to stop very, very slowly. If they stop too fast the logs keep moving and ram the tugs. Try pulling a wagon with a rope and then stop. You'll see what I mean.

We didn't make our tugboat stop at all. Big

Charlie cruised up beside it, matching its speed. Big Charlie flipped bumpers over the side of *The Golden Maiden* to protect his hull. Heavy Barry, who wasn't heavy at all and who worked as Big Charlie's crew, threw a couple of lines over to the tugboat crew. They cleated the lines and drew the two boats tightly together. A plank was laid out, complete with rails. Our bags and baseball equipment were thrown onto the tugboat deck and then we all walked the plank onto the tugboat.

It sounds simple. It is, actually, but it was still scary. The ocean seemed to breathe, in and out, pulling you down and pushing you up. The two boats seemed so small. It made your heart beat faster.

The lines between the boats were released, and Big Charlie pulled away from the tug, waving.

"Good luck!" he shouted, and then he blew his horn and we watched him head back toward the channel leading to our village.

Susan and I sat behind the wheelhouse, away from the wind. We watched the ocean for a couple of hours, hoping to see a pod of killer whales. It wasn't a smooth ride. Sometimes the ocean swells would push the logs a bit closer to the tugboat and the cable would relax, dropping into the ocean. Then the tug would surge forward and the cable would snap tight and pull back on the tug, jarring the whole boat.

I was glad we were sitting down.

"Do you know what amazes me when I'm out on a boat, Thumb?" said Susan. She had to shout over the noise of the engine. The tug was hauling a lot of weight, and the engine was working hard.

"What?"

"It's the sky."

"The sky?"

"Yeah. Our village is surrounded by mountains. We hardly ever get a chance to see much sky. The sky is so big and beautiful."

"Did you know that people who live where there are no mountains think that mountains are scenic and exciting?"

"Really? Mountains are just ordinary to me. But the sky, now that's scenic." Susan stared at the sky for a few minutes and then, still staring, said, "Big Charlie yelled good luck after dropping us off."

"I heard."

"Do you think he meant good luck with the baseball games?"

"He knows we can't win. These other teams are champions in their leagues. We've never even played." I shrugged. "He just wants us to have a good trip. That's all."

"But he said good luck."

"Maybe good luck means try not to lose by 43-0 in only two innings."

"I feel like we're on one of those television shows you see in the movies, where you have to do something really embarrassing to win a prize. We get a trip, but we have to play a game we've never played in our lives, against good teams who are going to laugh at us."

"Susan?"

"Yeah?"

"You're the one who insisted we have a team. We could still forfeit."

"I know. I just wish we could keep one game

really, really close. I wish we could be a real team for just one inning."

I looked around to make sure nobody was listening.

"Susan?" I said. "We've been practicing a lot. What if we're good? What if we could win a game?"

Susan turned and just looked at me.

"I've been reading a lot about baseball," I said. "Did you know that teams win way more often when their good pitchers throw? A team with a great pitcher just has to get a couple of runs because the other team isn't scoring. Any team can win if it has one good player, a pitcher. We need somebody with a pitch that the other team can't hit."

"You haven't read the tournament rules, Thumb. They don't want kids to get injuries by throwing too much. No player can pitch for more than four innings."

"So?" I said. "It just means we need two good pitchers. You and me."

"Us?"

"Yes. You're the best rock skipper. I'm not as

good as you but I'm the second best in the village. We'll be the best pitchers. We just have to believe in ourselves. We have to be confident that we can throw strikes that nobody can hit."

Mr. Entwhistle walked up to us and stopped.

"I wonder if I might see the two of you over by the side of the boat – that side – right away?"

"Sure," I said, glancing at Susan.

Mr. Entwhistle walked away from us slowly, leaning on his cane. On the lee side of the tugboat, he leaned against the rail, facing us with the ocean at his back. He glanced around to see if the three of us were alone.

"Ahem," he said slowly, clearing his throat. "I come, Thumb and Susan, from a seafaring nation. Britain was saved from the Spanish Armada by the strength of its navy. Britain was saved from Hitler by the strength of its navy. Britain became the most powerful nation on earth because it is surrounded by water."

He paused.

Susan and I didn't know what to say. We nodded.

"As the citizen of a nation whose very existence is based on its mastery of the waves and as a person whose very philosophy of life is Show No Fear, it is with great humiliation and with a plea for secrecy that I must ask you both to gather closely around me so that you might protect my privacy as I send my breakfast and my lunch into the bonny blue sea."

Mr. Entwhistle turned away from us and leaned over the side of the tugboat, making noises and sounds that Susan and I both recognized. We stood behind him and blocked anyone's view.

After a few minutes, he stopped and stood up.

"Thank you both," he said, pulling a cloth handkerchief from his pocket and dabbing at his mouth. "For a descendant of sailors, I have a surprisingly weak stomach. And here is a tip. When you find yourselves sick on a boat, always walk calmly to the side of the boat where the wind will blow whatever you eject from your body away from the boat and not back toward yourself. I discovered that the hard way."

The tugboat's horn blasted. It was so loud that we clasped our hands over our ears and looked around to see if a ship was in our way.

We ran to the other side of the tug. All of our teammates were staring into the distance.

"Look," said Susan, pointing. "It's Vancouver."

The high-rise buildings of Vancouver were coming into view as we passed an outstretched point of land. Vancouver's harbor was filled with hundreds of white sails and about a dozen tankers and cargo ships.

"Wow!" said Susan.

Another tug pulled alongside. The two tugs could actually lash themselves together since their huge rubber bumpers kept them from scraping each other. We climbed over to the harbor tug and it pulled away, heading back into the harbor, past sailboats and tankers.

We chugged under the Lion's Gate Bridge, stretched high above us. We could hear cars and trucks over the noise of the waves and the roar of the tugboat's engine.

Our tugboat pulled into a maze of wharves

and piers next to a huge glass building surrounded by people eating ice cream and drinking coffee as they watched the boats in the harbor. Dad had called ahead for a small bus, and
it sat waiting.

"We're going to ride in something with
wheels," Susan said, excited.

"Yeah," I said. "Of course."

"This is the first time. I'm actually going to
ride in something with wheels."

"But you knew we were going to do this."

"I knew it in my mind. Now I know it for
real. And I know something else, too."

"What?"

"It was a stupid idea for us to even try to
play baseball. The whole world here is just too
different."

7

The City

S USAN and I sat beside each other. The bus had to ride over the Lion's Gate Bridge. When the bus crossed the bridge, we couldn't see the road or even any railing, just the ocean below.

Susan gripped my arm and held tightly, although she still faced the window and the ocean.

"We're safe," I said, so quietly that nobody else would know she was scared. They were probably scared, too, I realized, since the conversations around us had stopped.

"This bridge has been standing for decades," I whispered.

"I'm scared on mountains," said Susan softly. "And they've been standing for millions of years."

Our hotel was the biggest building any of us

had ever been inside. Dad and Mr. Entwhistle checked us in and got our keys while we all stood behind them, staring up at the ceiling in the lobby. It was twice as high as the basketball court at home.

Dad gave us our keys. I was rooming with Robbie. Dad told us to gather in the lobby after we unpacked so that we could get something to eat and walk around the downtown. We took an elevator up to our floor. Even though it was Robbie's first elevator, he wasn't that excited.

"You just stand in a box and the doors shut and when the doors open you're on another floor. No big deal," said Robbie.

It wasn't even that exciting to look out the windows from the tenth floor. We'd both been on mountains and knew how it felt to stand on something tall and look down at the world.

Robbie picked the bed closest to the window and dropped his bag on top. He wanted to use the washroom right away. It was the first time he had ever used a toilet that flushed. He'd used water toilets on some of the fishing boats, but they were different.

Robbie spent a long time in the bathroom and then poked his head out.

"Did you know that the water in the shower is hot?" he asked. "Really hot? There's never this much hot water at home. Do you think I have time for a shower?"

"Sure," I said.

When we got down to the lobby, half our team was staring at the escalator up to the second floor. The other half was in line at the top, staring at the down escalator.

We had all seen escalators in movies but none of us, except for Dad and Mr. Entwhistle and me, had ridden one before.

Little Liam was at the front of the line, watching the steps as they came out of the floor. I could see Nick riding up the escalator, his hands on the moving rails. As soon as the step under him started to slide down flat, he leaped forward onto the flat and solid carpet of the second floor. He turned around and spread his arms wide, like he'd just sunk a winning basket two seconds before the final buzzer.

I walked over to the line and stood behind Susan. She looked at me and grinned.

"I never knew escalators were so noisy," she said. "Or so scary."

"Scary?"

"Yeah. I think we've each been up and down twice. Getting on isn't all that bad, although Little Liam is having a hard time. It's the getting off that's tricky. In the movies everyone just sort of walks right off, but it feels like that space between the steps is going to hook on your shoelace and suck you right under the floor. You've been on an escalator before, right?"

"Not for a few years."

"When people in books want to say that something's easy once you learn it, they always say that it's like riding a bike, but since I've never ridden a bike, that expression doesn't mean anything to me. Is riding an escalator like riding a bike? Do you still remember how?"

"I think so."

"Hey, guys," shouted Susan. "Let Thumb try. He's ridden an escalator before."

Susan pushed me up to the front of the line,

where Little Liam was still staring at the moving steps under him.

I looked at Little Liam and at everyone else. They all stared back at me, waiting.

"You just look down and step where there isn't a crack," I said. "If you do step on a crack, just scoot forward a bit. And when you get off, wait for the step to be almost flat and then step onto the floor. Watch."

I stepped easily onto the escalator and rode to the top. I stepped off, turned to the crowd below and bowed. My teammates cheered loudly.

Mr. Entwhistle suddenly stood beside me.

"Lads and lasses," he yelled. "May I have your attention, please?"

He waited for Big Bette to hop off the Up escalator before crossing his arms. "I think you have just learned a valuable lesson," he shouted. "Other teams are going to be able to catch and remember where to throw quite easily. These same tasks are going to seem difficult for you, just like riding this escalator. After all, you've never tried to hop off an escalator or complete a double play or catch a soaring fly ball. So, ride this escalator. All of you. Ride it four times or fourteen times or forty times. Ride it until you know that your bodies are relaxed. And tomorrow, when a fly ball is coming down at you, remember how much easier it is to do things when you are relaxed and confident. We're meeting outside for dinner in half an hour."

*   *   *

Once a year there was a community dinner in the New Auckland gym. It was in September on Firewood Day. Our houses were all heated with wood, so on Firewood Day our fishing boats cruised the edges of the bay, searching for fallen trees that could be reached easily. When a good dead tree was found, a couple of people hopped into a small aluminum boat with an outboard motor. The small boat dragged one end of a long chain or rope to the shore and the crew tied the rope around the tree. Then the fishing boat crew winched the tree into the ocean and hauled it back to the village where another crew in an aluminum boat untied it and hauled it up to the beach so that others could chop the tree into firewood. The wood was stacked on racks next to the sidewalk so that anyone could walk over with a wheelbarrow and take what they needed.

After the firewood was chopped up we had a big supper in the gym. The tables were pieces of plywood set on sawhorses. We tried not to have a basketball practice or game scheduled for the night before so that the gym didn't smell too much like sweat and dirty socks. It was a potluck dinner, although everybody pretty well knew what everybody else would bring.

I mention the dinner in the gym because it was about the only time that any of us ate around lots of people who weren't in our family.

We didn't go to a fancy restaurant, although we did have to wait to be seated, which was confusing to Big Bette. She kept pointing to empty tables and asking why we couldn't just go sit down.

We sat at three tables close together. Our table didn't even have an adult. We sort of knew what to do when the waiter came and stood beside us with a pad and paper but only because we'd seen lots of movies.

I ordered the roast chicken with fries and gravy. I also ordered a Coke. Robbie and Susan and Big Bette just nodded and said "the same" when the waitress looked at them.

"Whew," said Big Bette when the waitress left. "That was scary."

"Yeah," said Susan.

We looked around at the different tables. Some families were eating. Others were waiting for their food. Little Liam was inspecting the sugar packets on the table, frowning.

"What do we do now?" asked Robbie.

"We wait."

"They never wait in the movies."

"That's because it would be boring to watch people just wait for their meals."

"It's also boring to do. How long does it take?"

"I don't know. Around fifteen minutes. Why?"

"My parents call me when it's time to eat. I don't think I've ever just sat at a table and waited for dinner. Can't we go outside to play or something?"

"No. We just sit here."

"And wait?"

"And wait."

We sat and waited, with nobody saying a word. It took sixteen minutes and forty-three seconds, according to Susan. She was probably right.

After dinner, we walked back to the hotel. We had to cross three streets, one with a stoplight and a crosswalk button that we had to press so there would be enough time for us to cross on the green light. Big Bette thought the crosswalk button was the silliest thing she'd ever seen.

After we got back to the hotel, all the kids met in the room that Robbie and I shared. It was crowded, but we all fit.

"So," said Susan. "Here's the question. Are we going to try to play these games or are a couple of us going to get sick?"

"I'll get sick," offered Robbie. "I checked on the Internet and there's a miniatures store about ten blocks away. I could go there while the rest of you tour the city."

"I think we should play," I said.

"Why?" asked Nick.

"Because we are kids. Most of us have never played baseball and if we don't play now we never will."

"But look at all the things we can't do," said Little Liam. "I wanted a hamburger tonight at the restaurant but I just said 'the same' when the lady asked what I wanted to eat. I was too scared to say anything else. If I can't even order a meal, how can I play baseball?"

"I saw a baseball diamond in a park during the bus ride over here," said Big Bette. "It was the first time I've even seen a real baseball diamond. And tomorrow I'm supposed to play in a game?"

"Against champions," said Nick. "Not against kids like us, Thumb. Maybe, since you used to live in a city and can still remember how to ride escalators and order meals in restaurants, the idea of playing baseball doesn't seem so strange to you. But for me, it's terrifying. If we decide to play, I might just get sick for real."

I glanced at Susan.

"What do you think?" I asked.

"My mind says that it would be stupid for us to play, that we can't win. But something else inside me says that if we don't play then we're not going to have any fun in Vancouver tomorrow or the next day. It's like Erwin Schrödinger's cat."

"I don't know anybody named Schrödinger or even Erwin," said Robbie.

"Schrödinger was a physicist," said Susan, "but he is best known for a pretend experiment with a cat in a lead box. It's kind of a weird idea, but he said that, scientifically, we have to believe that the cat is both alive and dead until we open the box to peer inside. Schrödinger was trying to make some complicated point but here's what I got from it. We cannot assume that we will lose tomorrow. Anything is possible. There are two possibilities and neither is certain. In one future, we lose. In the other, we win."

"And in one we don't play," said Nick. "That's the future that's the easiest to handle. In that future, we know we don't embarrass ourselves."

"That's right," said Susan. "In one future we don't play. We don't open the box. We ignore it and put it on a shelf. I can't believe I'm saying this, but I have to open the box. I have to see if we can play baseball. I want to play baseball. I don't know why, but it's important."

"You know," said Robbie with a grin. "I'm feeling a little better already. I may not be sick after all."

We all looked around and grinned at each other.

"We're going to play baseball," said Nick with a sigh.

"Like real kids from a real town," said Susan softly.

After everyone left, Robbie and I couldn't sleep. We were excited. We were also in a hotel room with a television set.

We left the television on all night, with the sound turned low. We kept the TV tuned to a sports channel so maybe we'd learn something about baseball in our sleep.

8

The First Game

T HE next morning we left the hotel and stood at the corner waiting for a city bus — nine kids and two adults wearing baseball uniforms. Mr. Entwhistle had bought us uniforms and hats and given them to us at breakfast. On the back of each uniform was a picture from a different Bobbie and Bernice book. Mine had a picture of Bobbie and Bernice building the Leaning Tower of Pisa. Susan's had a picture of Bobbie building a giant sleigh, from the book where Santa's sleigh is overloaded and it crashes in the forest and Bobbie and Bernice have to build him another one so that all the kids in the world can get their presents. Mr. Entwhistle says it's the Bobbie and Bernice book that sells the best but the one he likes the least.

Four men and three women waited with us at the bus stop. They were probably going to work.

"Look, a police car!" yelled Little Liam.

We all turned to look, expecting the car to swerve to a stop and for the officers inside to race down the street chasing somebody. Most of us had never seen a police car except in movies and they were always chasing bad guys.

We waved at the car as it slowly passed us.

"And there's a man walking a dog on a leash," yelled Big Bette. The dog, a small white pile of fluff, strutted along with its head held high.

We all started laughing. The dogs in our village would probably pull you around the village three times if you tried to put a leash on them. But in New Auckland there are no cars and no place to go even if a dog did decide to run away. Besides, our dogs have to run free. They help keep skunks and other small animals away from the village.

There were eight different baseball diamonds at the park. We walked to number six. The team we were supposed to play was already out on the field, tossing balls and practicing. We couldn't believe how far they could throw and hit.

The coach from the other team jogged over to Dad. He was a tall man with a bushy brown moustache.

"I'm Mr. Darling of the Kamloops Kangaroos," he said to Dad. "And, hey, I know there are no kangaroos in Kamloops. Somebody just thought the two words sounded good together. You're the team from up the coast?"

"Yes," said Dad. "I'm Mr. Mazzei. I'm the coach."

Mr. Darling moved a clipboard so he could shake hands with Dad. Mr. Darling wasn't looking at Dad, though. He was looking at our team.

Robbie was putting on the catcher's pads upside down. Big Bette was standing beside Dad, her uniform top so long that it looked like a dress on her. Nick and Little Liam were rolling in the grass and rubbing it with their hands. Susan and I were pulling at our uniforms, trying to feel more comfortable.

"We've just about finished warming up if you want to practice now," said Mr. Darling from Kamloops.

"Actually," said Dad, "why don't you folks

carry on for a little while longer? We're not quite organized yet."

Dad didn't say that the reason we wanted the Kamloops team to practice longer was so that we could see what to do when we were out on the field. We were pretty sure we understood the rules. We'd rented every baseball movie possible and watched them each about five times. We mostly watched them to see where people stood and what they did.

The stories were always the same. Some team had no skill but managed to win the big game anyway. A small kid with glasses usually made the big catch or hit the ball after having struck out every other time.

The movies taught us a lot. We knew how to look cool. We knew how to glance casually and calmly at the coach for a sign about where or how to hit the ball. We knew to stare at the pitcher so he'd get nervous.

We knew everything except how to hit and catch and where to stand and what a sign from the coach might look like and where to throw if we ever did manage to catch anything.

"Sure," said Coach Darling, glancing at our uniforms and smiling. "So, you guys are the Northern Coast League champs, eh?"

"We're undefeated," said Susan.

"Hey, aren't those pictures from the Bobbie and Bernice books on your uniforms? My son, our third baseman, he loved those books when he was little."

"Yeah," said Dad. "Our team is called the Beavers and Mr. Entwhistle, who writes and illustrates the Bobbie and Bernice books, lives in our village. Actually, he's right over there," said Dad, pointing toward the street, where Mr. Entwhistle was inspecting a rose bush.

Mr. Darling glanced over at Mr. Entwhistle and then slowly looked at each of us. He wasn't really sure yet if we were a bad team or a really good team trying to psych him out.

Robbie was trying to shove his mitt on the wrong hand.

"Remember, Robbie," said Susan calmly. "You put the glove on your left hand so that you can use your right hand for throwing."

"But I still think it's more important for me

to catch the ball first. I have a better chance of catching the ball if the glove is on my right hand."

"Mr. Mazzei, do we all get to wear these?" asked Big Bette, holding up a catcher's mask. We didn't have a catcher's mask in our school kit but Dad had bought one after dinner last night.

"No, Bette," said Dad softly, taking the catcher's mask from her. "The only person who wears a mask is the one who catches the balls that the pitcher throws."

"But any of us could get hit in the face."

"The catcher has the highest chance of getting hit, Bette."

"Then can I be the catcher? I'd like to wear the mask."

"The catcher has to be able to catch," said Dad calmly.

"Oh," said Bette, tossing the mask back onto our pile of equipment.

Dad turned to face Coach Darling. "You play with the mercy rule, don't you?"

"The mercy rule?"

"Yeah. If one team is leading by more than ten runs after two innings, then the game is declared over without the rest of the game being played."

"I suppose we use that rule if it's in the book," said Coach Darling slowly. "It's never happened, though."

"Well, it will probably happen today," said Dad.

Coach Darling nodded. He smiled sympathetically at us and jogged back toward his team. He pulled out a whistle and blew it, gathering his team together.

Dad seemed to think it was a good idea to give us a pep talk, too. He didn't have to call his team together. We were all sitting and lying on the grass, rubbing it and looking at it.

"I suppose," said Dad, "that I should tell you how we might be able to win if we concentrate. But the truth is that we don't even know what to concentrate on. Each of you should pick the player that is stationed at your position in the field and watch that player closely. Copy what that player does. When we're out on the field and a ball is hit toward you, try not to let it get past you. If you can't catch it, just stop it. If you happen to hit the ball when it's your turn to bat, then first base is to the right and not to the left the way it is at home. Run to first base and stop. If Mr. Entwhistle tells you to run to second base, go — fast. That's it. Remember, have fun. Now, let's play some baseball!"

We got to bat first, which was great since everyone who wasn't batting could watch the kids in the field and see what they were doing.

Big Bette went up to the plate, carrying a huge bat on her shoulder. The fielders moved in close, thinking that if Big Bette did hit the ball it sure wouldn't go far.

The players from Kamloops started to yell things at Big Bette, saying she couldn't hit and looked too weak to even swing the bat.

"Hey!" yelled Susan. "Be nice! That's our friend up there and she can't help it if she's small!"

"Susan," said Dad without turning his head. "Yeah?"

"What they're doing is part of the game.

They're trying to rattle the batter. They can do that. All teams do that. When they're batting, they'll yell at our pitcher. It's part of baseball."

"I memorized the rules," said Susan, "and that is not in there at all."

"Trust me, they can do it," said Dad.

"So we can make up insults and yell at their team?" asked Robbie. "Why didn't you tell us?"

Robbie cupped his hands and yelled out toward the pitcher, "Hey, you on the pitcher's mound. How can you throw with all that snot hanging out your nose?"

The pitcher threw a ball over Bette's head. Her bat stayed on her shoulder. He didn't throw the ball high because of what Robbie said. He threw it high because Big Bette's head wasn't all that far from the ground. Bette stood in a slight crouch to make her strike zone even smaller.

"Ball one!" yelled the umpire.

"Come on, pitcher! You couldn't tell the difference between a strike zone and a crossing zone!"

"Robbie," said Dad softly.

"Yeah?" asked Robbie.

"I know it is all right to shout insults. Still, I would try to be a little less provocative."

"What does provocative mean?"

"It means likely to make the other team angry."

"Why can't I be provocative?"

"Because Bette will probably get on base but this Kamloops team is going to beat us very, very badly. Never show fear but never provoke a sleeping lion, either."

"Take your base!" yelled the umpire.

Big Bette stood at home plate, the bat on her shoulder.

"He walked you," yelled Dad. "You can go to first base."

Big Bette nodded and dropped her bat. She started jogging toward third base.

"You know that first base is over there," yelled Dad, pointing.

"Right," said Big Bette as casually as she could. She jogged across the infield to stand at first base with her hands on her knees. We could see the Kamloops players look at each other, puzzled.

Nick came up to bat. He held his bat above his shoulder and glared at the pitcher. He swung at the first three pitches and missed them all.

The next two batters struck out, too, and it was time for the Kamloops team to hit.

I ran out to the field, pulling on my glove. I took my position, hands on my knees, focused and ready and praying that nobody hit a ball toward me. I figured that if I looked mean and acted like I knew what I was doing then maybe the batters would try to hit the ball somewhere else.

Nick pitched. Dad figured that Nick was our best athlete and that he would pitch the hardest and the fastest.

Maybe so, but the Kamloops Kangaroos seemed to like hard and fast pitches. Kamloops scored eight runs in the first inning. We got somebody out when a runner should have stayed at first but tried for a double. We got another out when Little Liam caught a fly ball and the third on a strikeout. When Nick got his strikeout we all cheered and ran out to hug him like we'd won the World Series.

"Hey, at least you got plenty of practice out

there," said Dad as we ran to the dugout. "And you all have a better idea of where to throw the ball when there's a hit."

It was my turn to bat.

"Remember what I said," whispered Dad. "You'll never hit the ball very far if you just use your arms. You have to twist your shoulders and use your whole body."

I nodded and walked up to the batter's box. I tapped the plate with my bat several times like I had seen some of the other players do. I glared at the pitcher, held the bat above my shoulder and waited for the first pitch. I didn't swing when it came, mostly because it hit the catcher's glove before I even thought about swinging.

"Strike one," yelled the umpire.

I swung at the next pitch and hit it foul. It felt good to hit something. I watched one of the fielders casually walk over, pick up the ball and toss it back to the pitcher.

I hit the third pitch over the second baseman's head and ran to first base for a hit.

The team cheered, of course, and Mr. Entwhistle gave me a pat on the shoulder.

"Do you want to try to steal second?" he whispered.

"What do I do?"

"The next time the pitcher starts his wind-up, you start running for second. Slide when you get close."

I waited and ran when it felt right. I would have made it, too, if I hadn't started my slide too early, head down and arms extended toward second base. If my arms and fingers were three times as long I still wouldn't have reached the bag. The second baseman had to walk over to me before he bent down and tagged me.

"You're out!" yelled the umpire.

I felt ridiculous and didn't even want to stand up. I was hoping the cloud of dust would hover, hiding me for as long as possible.

We lost sixteen to nothing in two innings.

When the game was over, Dad walked over to shake hands with Mr. Darling from the other team.

"Your kids have never played baseball before, have they?" asked Mr. Darling.

"No," said Dad. "Playing in this tournament

was the only way I could get the school board to let me bring them to Vancouver."

"Tell you what," said Mr. Darling, looking back at us. "The ball diamond's still free. What if my team gives your team some lessons?"

"Could they?"

"Sure. Hey," said Mr. Darling with a laugh, "maybe we can help you actually win your next game. It could happen. Who are you playing?"

"Vancouver."

"Oh," said Mr. Darling.

9

Why Not?

I UNDERSTOOD most inventions. I knew planes could fly because I'd seen them in the air. Besides, we studied airplanes in school. We learned how the curve of the wing creates lift, with the air moving faster across the bottom of the wing.

It was also easy for me to understand how a room could be heated because in New Auckland, we cut down trees and chopped up logs. We put logs in cast-iron fireplaces and lit them and felt the temperature rise.

I even understood how refrigerators work. We had a refrigerator, run by a generator.

But what I couldn't understand was how the air in an entire hotel could be chilled with air-conditioning, creating huge indoor spaces that were colder than it was outside.

At home, Dad got mad at me when I left the

refrigerator door open, telling me how I was wasting energy and saying things like, "What are you trying to do, cool the whole house?" But nobody seemed to think it was wasting energy to cool huge indoor spaces in cities.

We saw enormous bridges and buildings. We rode the Skytrain, which was pretty exciting, and we saw endless rows of houses and sidewalks filled with people and thousands of cars and trucks, all of which made noise.

But it was the little things that surprised us the most.

We weren't used to seeing strangers. Each of us knew the name of every person in New Auckland and knew when each person had been sick or done something brave, like when Robbie's dad picked up a distress signal on his radio and took his boat out in a storm to save some amateur sailor. It bothered us to walk down Vancouver streets and not be able to stare at each person's face and really know that person.

Big Bette saw her first horse. We all saw it, of course, but Big Bette screamed when the policeman and his horse trotted around a corner, heading toward us. Big Bette wasn't expecting to see a horse in the city.

The policeman stopped and told us the horse's name was Jubilee. He was a big brown horse with a black mane. Big Bette tried to pat him on the head but she couldn't reach. The policeman whistled once and the horse stomped one foot and lowered his head. Big Bette rubbed his neck and stared deeply into his eyes.

"My trip," she said with a sigh, "is perfect."

We went to eat at a place that served huge burgers, with French fries that came wrapped in grease-soaked newspaper to keep them hot.

At dinner we all talked about the game. We sat at our tables with our mitts on our laps and when we weren't eating we'd sort of slip a hand inside and punch the pocket so it felt like a baseball smacking into the glove.

Mr. Entwhistle ate a hamburger just like the rest of us, but he ate it with a knife and fork, cutting the burger into pieces and chewing slowly. None of us laughed, but we all stared when he wasn't looking. Mr. Entwhistle talked about how we had played and how we could play better. It took him a while to say anything since he didn't believe in talking when he had any food in his mouth. He'd say about a sentence while he was cutting his hamburger and then he'd stop while he chewed and swallowed.

"Mr. Darling, the coach from the other team," said Mr. Entwhistle, "told me that Susan and Thumb tossed the most unusual pitches in practice. These pitches are not fast and they don't curve terribly far, but Susan and Thumb can toss them sidearm with spin. The Vancouver batters will be as disturbed by the strange wind-up as you were by the escalator. And even when a batter hits one of these odd pitches, there is an excellent chance that the ball will spin out of bounds. He is thankful that Susan and Thumb did not pitch against his team."

"He thinks we can win a game?" asked Susan.

Mr. Entwhistle shrugged. "Anything is possible," he said. "I am a classic example of that statement. I once wanted to be a painter.

Instead, here I am living in a fishing village on the edge of the world coaching baseball, a game I have never had the honor to play. As you will see when you grow up, anything can happen and often does. You can certainly win. It's a game."

"What's the other team like?" asked Robbie.

"They're the Vancouver champions," said Dad. "They don't lose many games. They're big. They're strong. They have a terrific hitter named Jack Sachmo. They have a couple of good pitchers but I don't think they'll use them against us. They'll save their best pitchers for other teams."

"Do we have a chance?"

"Probably not," said Dad. "But I can tell you that the other team's players are absolutely sure they can beat us. If we scare them and scare them early, they might panic and try too hard. Can we win? Why not?"

10

The Second Game

W E actually warmed up before our second game, throwing the ball back and
forth and swinging the bat.

"Play ball!" yelled the umpire.

Susan turned and looked at me. She actually
grinned. She looked back at Robbie, who stood
next to second base, and then over at Big Bette
and the others. We were all grinning. I reached
down with my bare hand and rubbed the grass
for luck and tried to remember to breathe.

Little Liam was our catcher. He crouched
down low and held out his glove as a target.

Susan twirled the ball in her hands until she
got a good grip on the seams. She pulled her
arm back sideways, like she was getting ready to
skip a stone on the ocean. She threw the ball,
and it curved away from home plate and then
veered straight for the batter. He fell to the

ground. The ball bounced out of Little Liam's mitt and spun on the ground like a top.

"Ball one!" yelled the umpire.

The batter brushed himself off and glared at Susan. Susan looked back at me and made a face. I walked slowly over to her.

"I can do the height just fine," said Susan, "but it's hard to get the ball to go right over the plate. I'll get it in a couple of pitches."

"You scared the batter. That's good," I said.

I smiled and walked back to first base, putting my hands on my knees again.

Susan threw another curving pitch that quickly veered toward the batter. He ducked.

"Strike one!" yelled the umpire.

Susan looked back at me and wiggled her eyebrows.

She struck out the first three batters, and our team ran excitedly to the bench, hugging each other like we'd won the game.

"They didn't score one run," said Robbie.

"They didn't even get a hit," said Big Bette, grabbing a bat and a helmet and heading to the batter's box.

The Vancouver pitcher walked her, of course.

Dad came and sat beside me.

"Watch this," he said. "She's going to steal second base on the second pitch."

"But she's not that fast," I said.

"She doesn't have to be," said Dad. "Surprise. That's what we're after."

Nick took the first pitch, a strike.

The Vancouver pitcher reared back and threw his second pitch. Big Bette ran toward second base. She galloped on all fours, like she did when she was pretending to be a horse.

The catcher caught the ball and just stood, watching. Everyone did. The stands were quiet.

The umpire stood watching, too. Big Bette stood on second base and brushed off her hands.

"Safe!" yelled the umpire.

Nick struck out and so did Little Liam.

I was the next batter and I got a hit. I'd love to say that there was some skill involved but the truth is that I closed my eyes when I swung the bat and was surprised when the bat sort of shuddered in my hands and made a noise that was the most wonderful sound I had ever heard.

I opened my eyes, wondering if the ball had gone fair or foul.

"Run," yelled everyone on my team, so I did. And so did Big Bette. She ran to third like a normal person and then ran home on all fours. She was safe. We had scored our first run, and we were leading.

Robbie struck out. The bat never left his shoulder. Robbie said that he was afraid of swinging, afraid that he'd look silly, even though he didn't know anybody in Vancouver and knew that we wouldn't laugh at him. The inning was over. We were ahead, 1 to 0.

Susan stood on the pitcher's mound and faced the best hitter on the Vancouver team. Jack Sachmo had announced to anyone within hearing that he intended to be a big league baseball player. He was already deciding what products he wanted to endorse. Jack watched Susan throw two pitches, both strikes, without swinging his bat. He watched the way the pitch left

her arm and the way it curved and where it passed over the plate.

He hit the third pitch so far that it may still be up in the sky. Jack rounded the bases and ran back to the Vancouver dugout. The game was tied.

Jack started talking to his teammates, pointing to Susan and to home plate. We knew what he was doing. Jack had figured out that all of Susan's pitches followed the same pattern. If the Vancouver batters knew the pattern, they could hit her pitch every time. I jogged over to the pitcher's mound and so did Dad.

"Good pitchers have more than one pitch," said Dad.

"Well, I don't," said Susan.

"Do your best," said Dad and he trotted back to our dugout. The rest of us ran back to our positions, more attentive now. We knew balls would be hit to us. And they were. By the time we got the Vancouver team out, they were leading 5 to 1.

We didn't score any runs during our turn to bat.

"Well," said Susan gloomily as another batter struck out. "We're not going to lose by the mercy rule. We have to play the whole seven innings."

"That means we're playing better than we were yesterday," I said.

"It won't look that way on paper," said Susan. "The Vancouver players have figured out my pitch and they'll figure out that you're throwing pretty much the same way. They'll score so many runs that we'll wish the game could have stopped after two innings."

"Actually," I said softly, "maybe Dad is wrong. Maybe you don't need more than one pitch."

"What do you mean?"

"What if you throw the same pitch but throw it in different places?"

"I don't get it."

"What if you don't always try to throw strikes? The batters know where to swing. What if some of your pitches miss the plate on purpose? What if the ball is lower or higher or so close to them that they have to think about ducking? They think you only throw strikes, so they're swinging at everything."

Susan looked at me and grinned.

Susan struck out all three Vancouver batters. When it was our turn to bat Nick hit a home run. The score was 5 to 2.

The Vancouver team did get three hits off Susan in the fourth inning but we stopped them from scoring. We didn't score any runs when it was our turn to bat.

"Fifth inning," said Dad. "By the rules, we have to change pitchers. That means you, Thumb."

A new pitcher gets eight warm-up pitches. I didn't throw any sidearm, rock-skipping pitches during my warm-up. All eight times I tried to throw like a normal pitcher, with a leg lift and a weight shift and an overhead, almost straight-arm toss of the baseball. None of my warm-up pitches were very good and I could see the Vancouver batters smile at each other. They figured they'd faced our one good pitcher and now they got to hit and hit and hit.

I pitch left-handed while Susan pitches right-handed. My curving, twisting, rock-skipping sidearm pitch seemed to come straight toward a right-handed batter and then to curve away at the last moment.

I struck out the first two batters I faced.

Then Jack Sachmo stepped up to the plate. He'd been watching, and he was ready, except I didn't throw him the same pitch. I didn't use the seams to make the ball spin. I just threw it sidearm so that it looked the same as all of my other pitches, but it didn't curve at all. It went straight, not even close to home plate. It wasn't a fast pitch, and Jack might have hit it if it had curved. Instead, he swung through the place he expected the ball to be and missed.

"Strike one," yelled the umpire.

I threw my curve next but threw it low, so that it was barely above Jack's shins when it passed home plate. He swung and missed again.

"Strike two," yelled the umpire.

I didn't even try to throw a strike with my third pitch. I threw a curve that would cross inside the plate, close to Jack. He ducked.

"Ball one," said the umpire, holding up his fingers.

I struck Jack out with a regular curve, and he didn't even swing.

It was our turn to bat.

We scored a run, too. Little Liam hit a ball so far that I think he rounded the bases before it landed. The score was 5 to 3. Two more innings to play.

I struck out two batters and Big Bette actually caught a fly ball. Vancouver didn't score any runs.

We did. Big Bette walked. The pitcher was so worried that Big Bette might drop to all four legs and start running that he tossed a slow pitch to Nick who hit it solidly and managed a double. Big Bette had to stop at third base. Little Liam got a hit and Big Bette ran home. Nick ran to third. We were only one run behind.

I struck out.

Robbie came up to bat.

"Easy out," shouted the Vancouver first baseman. Several Vancouver players picked up the chant. Robbie stepped out of the batter's box. Dad walked over and whispered something to him. Robbie nodded and stepped back into the batter's box, tapping his bat several times against the plate, hard.

The Vancouver pitcher almost lobbed the ball to Robbie, daring him to swing. Robbie leaned back on his right leg and swung the bat as he shifted his weight forward.

He hit the ball hard. It would not have been a home run if Little Liam or Nick had been at bat, since the fielders would have been playing deep. But every Vancouver outfielder was playing close, figuring that if Robbie did hit the ball then he wouldn't hit it very far.

They were wrong. The ball flew over the center fielder's head. Nick scored and so did Little Liam and Robbie. We all leaped off the bench and hugged Robbie as he crossed home plate, laughing.

"What did my dad say to you?" I asked him.

"He told me that I spent about a month every fall chopping firewood with an ax about the same size as a baseball bat, and that I could swing an ax as well as anybody. He said that I should just pretend that I was swinging an ax, but level, like when I chop down a tree. He's right. It's the same motion."

We didn't score any more runs. One inning left to play, and we were leading by two. If we could get three Vancouver batters out before they could tie the game or take the lead, we'd win.

Dad handed me the ball as I slipped on my mitt.

Susan walked out to the pitcher's mound beside me.

"If we win then we have to play another game," said Susan, reminding me.

"So?" I said. "Do you want me to throw soft pitches?"

"No. But I don't want to play again, either. Even if we lose we can go home proud. I just worry what might happen if we play another game."

"If we lose, we lose, Susan. But we can win. Can you imagine? We can win. Sometimes, Susan, you think too much. Let's just enjoy what's happening right now."

I checked my players and threw to the first

batter, striking him out on four pitches. I looked over at the bleachers. Mr. Darling, the coach of the Kamloops team, stood up and clapped so that I'd see him. I tipped the brim of my hat, like I'd seen heroes do in western movies.

I threw a sidearm pitch to the next Vancouver batter, who got a hit and managed to make it to second base when Nick held the ball too long, not quite sure where to throw it.

The next batter struck out, but the Vancouver runner managed to steal third base.

I walked the next batter, and then Jack Sachmo came up to bat. If Jack got a hit, any kind of a hit, then two runners would score and Vancouver would tie the game. If he got a home run, Vancouver would win.

Jack watched the first pitch, a strike. I threw a ball that looked almost the same but was lower. Jack watched it and the umpire called out, "Ball one!"

Jack hit my third pitch, a soft, short hopper right to me. He ran toward first base. One Vancouver runner raced for home and the other ran toward third, ready to keep running. I caught the ball and turned toward Susan. I sidearm-tossed her the baseball. I knew when I threw it that the toss was fast enough and accurate enough to reach first base well before Jack. I knew that if Susan caught the ball then the game was over and we had won. I knew that nobody would blame Susan if she dropped the ball since we all dropped a lot of balls and none of us had ever tried to catch a ball with so much cheering and noise and pressure.

It seemed like the ball and Jack were both moving in slow motion. Susan reached out with her glove, staring at the ball as it came closer and closer. The ball hit her glove, and she squeezed tightly. She glanced down to make sure her foot was touching first base just as Jack ran past her.

"You're out!" yelled the first base umpire.

The New Auckland Beavers had defeated the Vancouver champs.

I jumped up and down and, with the rest of the team, I ran over to first base and hugged Susan.

"You caught it," I whispered in her ear.

"Yeah," she said. "We won, Thumb. We won."

11

Home

W E forfeited our last game. I sat on the bed in Dad's room while he called the tournament organizers. He winked at me as he told them that three of our players had the flu.

It was the first time I'd ever heard Dad tell a lie.

"You told a lie," I said, surprised.

"Just a little one."

"It was still a lie."

"It was a noble lie, like when you tell a proud mother that her ugly baby is beautiful. Mind you, if I ever catch you lying, I'll wash your mouth out with soap," Dad said, laughing. "Now let's go downstairs and join our team."

We didn't have to catch the tugboat heading north until late in the afternoon. Dad asked us what we wanted to do. I was tempted to say that I wanted to stay in the hotel room and watch television.

"I was going to ask if I could go to the miniatures store," said Robbie, "but I'd rather do something with the whole team. Can we go to a movie? One in a theater with a huge screen and a good sound system."

"Yeah," said the rest of the team members.

"But don't you want to do something outside?" asked Dad.

"We've seen big tall buildings and lots of cars and roads and trains and things," said Robbie. "Can we just go to a movie? Please? We've never seen a movie on a big screen."

So we did. We went to see *The Knights of the Tower*. It was the most amazing thing I have ever watched in my life. I sat still for three hours as heroes and villains and battles and wars and dangers took place on a screen that was so big and bright and loud and alive that I knew that some day I would live in a city again.

"Leon?" said Mr. Entwhistle on the tugboat as we headed back home. "When are you going to take off your thumb for me, lad? I'd love to see how this contraption of yours works."

"Not on the boat. I might drop it and then it

might roll overboard. I'll do it as soon as we get back," I promised.

When we were close to our village, Big Charlie's fishing boat, decorated with banners and flags, pulled next to the tugboat and we all crossed over. We waved goodbye to the tugboat captain and crew and pulled away, heading for the gap between the mountains where New Auckland lay hidden from view.

We rounded Linda Evers Mountain. The beach was lined with villagers, cheering and waving. Five small motorboats weaved around us, waiting to take us to the dock so that we could all arrive together.

"There's a little ceremony planned for the gym," said Annie Pritchard as I stepped onto the dock.

"But we just won one game. It was no big deal."

"I know," said Annie. "We're all proud but the real reason we want to bring everyone into the gym is that this is the perfect excuse for all of us to be together when you take off your thumb for Mr. Entwhistle." She was grinning.

"Do you have the box I carved for you?"

"Yeah. It's in my gym bag."

"Perfect. Let's go."

The team lined up across the middle of the gym floor. The stands were filled with our mothers and fathers and brothers and sisters and friends. I knew everyone.

Big Charlie, our mayor when we needed one, made a short speech about how the mighty New Auckland team had defeated the Vancouver all-stars in a game of baseball, a game that required grass and a huge playing field.

One of the reasons Big Charlie was our mayor was that we didn't have a speaker system. Big Charlie's voice was so loud that he didn't need one. Another reason was that Big Charlie's speeches were always short.

Big Charlie invited everyone to cheer again, louder.

"Now," said Big Charlie, rubbing his hands together. "One of the two coaches of our fine baseball team is an Englishman who never even saw a game of baseball before traveling down to

Vancouver with our kids. Come on up here, Mr. Entwhistle."

Mr. Entwhistle walked over to Big Charlie.

"Actually," he whispered to Big Charlie, "I've seen a few baseball games."

"Doesn't make any difference," Big Charlie whispered back. "It's a better tale if you've never seen a game."

"Mr. Entwhistle," shouted Big Charlie to the crowd, "has been wanting to see Thumb take off his thumb. What do you say, Thumb? Would you do it now, please?"

The crowd cheered but nobody smiled or leaned over to whisper to a neighbor. They knew that you could only sell a joke if the person you were planning to fool didn't think they were about to be tricked.

I reached into my gym bag and pulled out the box that Annie Pritchard had carved. There was a carving of Raven on top. Raven is the trickster for most of the native people that live along the coast.

I walked forward and stood beside Mr. Entwhistle.

Mr. Entwhistle stared down at the box. He stared hard.

"That box," he said. "It's beautiful."

"Annie carved it for me. Well, for my thumb," I said, trying to keep my voice normal.

"Annie can carve?"

"I've never seen her carve anything except this box, but she sure did a good job so I guess she can carve pretty well."

If Mr. Entwhistle had any thoughts that my thumb might be some sort of practical joke, the box seemed to convince him that I really could take off my thumb. The box was a work of art. He didn't ask to hold it, which was good, since it had a hole in the bottom where I stuck my thumb when I pretended to take it off. But he did stare at the box, putting his face as close as he could and admiring the details.

I wiggled all my fingers and my thumb and then reached into my pocket for the small screwdriver I kept there. I showed Mr. Entwhistle the screwdriver and then turned my back to him. I pretended to unscrew tiny little screws on each side of my thumb. I slipped the screwdriver back into my pocket, and then slid my thumb into the hole in the bottom of the box, adjusting the cotton at the bottom so that Mr. Entwhistle couldn't tell that my thumb was still attached.

I closed the lid, turned around and faced Mr. Entwhistle, holding the box so that he and I were standing side by side in front of the bleachers. I took a deep breath and opened the lid.

Mr. Entwhistle leaned over to take a good look at my thumb. He stared at the thumb and at the cotton underneath. Big Charlie moved up so that he could catch Mr. Entwhistle if he fainted.

I waited a couple of seconds. I even glanced up and grinned at the audience while Mr. Entwhistle inspected my thumb closely.

I winked at the audience, and then I wiggled my thumb.

The idea, of course, was that Mr. Entwhistle was supposed to scream or faint or leap into the air or do something funny that we could all laugh about for weeks.

Mr. Entwhistle stayed motionless, bent over

the box. He reached into his pocket and pulled out his leather glasses case, opened it and slipped his glasses on his nose so that he could take a closer look.

I frowned and wiggled my thumb again, nodding toward the audience so that they'd know what I was doing. Mr. Entwhistle rubbed his chin, like Sherlock Holmes figuring out some clue. He thought for a moment and then leaned way over so that he could see the bottom of the box and the hole.

He stood up and laughed.

"Oh, that is a good one, Thumb. You almost scared me to death. You did. What a terrific little joke. I love it. Wiggle it again. My word. I have never been so frightened in all my life."

"You sure didn't look that frightened," said Big Charlie.

"I never show fear," said Mr. Entwhistle. "I'm English."

* * *

I have my own children now. We go back to New Auckland each summer and stay in Mr.

Entwhistle's old cottage with its rounded doors and cedar floors. Mr. Entwhistle retired to England after he wrote his last tale about Bobbie and Bernice Beaver.

Every summer I take my kids into the school in New Auckland and show them a small trophy in a glass case there. A golden baseball player stands on top of that trophy, gazing out toward an invisible pitcher. His bat is off his shoulders, poised to swing.

There's a plaque on the base of the trophy. It says Sixth Place. Provincial Middle School Baseball Championships. Our single victory earned us sixth place for a team from a village without grass or a field large enough to hit a ball.

We didn't even know that we were going to get a trophy. It arrived by seaplane, of course. Each team member got to take it home for an entire night before it made its way to the trophy case.

My son and my daughter play baseball on a team in the city. They like it but I doubt if they get the same shivers of fear and excitement that the New Auckland Beavers felt when they played.

They do reach down and rub their hands through the grass for luck just before each game, though. It's a family tradition.